# Farmers

Sandy Sepehri

Bethany, Missouri

Photo Credits:
Cover © NRCS/Norm Klopfenstein, NRCS/Bob Nichols;  Title Page © Dale Stork;  Page 4 © Sia Chen How;
Page 5 © Michael West;  Page 7 © Christy Thompson;  Page 8 © USDA;  Page 9 © Neil Roy Johnson;
Page 10 © Joe Gough;  Page 11 © Lenice Harms;  Page 12 © L. Bakker;  Page 15 © Scott Slattery;
Page 17 © Tony Campbell;  Page 19 © Jan Matoska;  Page 20 © Cameron Pushak;  Page 21 © Elena Kalistratova;
Page 22 © Elena Aliaga

Cataloging-in-Publication Data

Sepehri, Sandy
    Farmers / Sandy Sepehri. — 1st ed.
    p. cm. — (Community helpers)

    Includes bibliographical references and index.
    Summary:  Text and photographs introduce different kinds
of farmers and what they do, what they bring to our homes,
tools they use, and more.
    ISBN-13:  978-1-4242-1353-5 (lib. bdg. : alk. paper)
    ISBN-10:  1-4242-1353-3 (lib. bdg. : alk. paper)
    ISBN-13:  978-1-4242-1443-3 (pbk. : alk. paper)
    ISBN-10:  1-4242-1443-2 (pbk. : alk. paper)

    1. Farmers—Juvenile literature.  2. Farm life—Juvenile literature.
3. Agriculture—Juvenile literature.
4. Agriculture—Vocational guidance—Juvenile literature.
[1. Farmers.  2. Farm life.  3. Agriculture.  4. Agriculture—Vocational guidance.
5. Occupations.]  I. Sepehri, Sandy.  II. Title.  III. Series.
    S519.S47 2007
    630—dc22

First edition
© 2007 Fitzgerald Books
802 N. 41st Street, P.O. Box 505
Bethany, MO  64424, U.S.A.
Printed in China
Library of Congress Control Number:  2007900211

# Table of Contents

# What Do Farmers Do?

    Farmers make three important things.
First, they make food by growing **crops**
and tending animals.

Secondly, they help make clothes by growing fiber crops, like cotton. Thirdly, they help make fuel that comes from sugarcane, corn, and other grains.

# What Do Farmers Bring to Our Homes?

Most homes have many things that a farmer helped make. Cookies, bread, ice cream—even pancake syrup and soda—have ingredients that come from farms. Bed sheets, curtains, leather shoes, and furniture are also made of things that come from farms.

# The First Farmers

Thousands of years ago people learned that plants grow from seeds, so they grew their own food and became farmers.

By having farms, people no longer had to hunt animals for food. They built towns and learned how to use animals to pull their plows.

# Different Kinds of Farmers

Crop farmers grow and **harvest** fruits, vegetables, grains, and fibers such as cotton.

Cattle farmers raise **livestock** and sell the meat from their animals. Fish farmers raise fish for food, bait, and pets.

Dairy farmers use machines to pump milk from cows. Other dairy products are butter, cheese, yogurt, and ice cream.

Poultry farmers raise fowl for both their eggs and their meat. Chicken, turkeys, and ducks are poultry.

# Careers in Farming

Some farmers own family farms and some work for large farms called agribusinesses. Others are farm managers, agricultural engineers, agricultural consultants, or agricultural scientists.

15

# The Farmers' Tools

Modern farms use many machines. Tractors pull plows and reapers. Plows prepare the ground for seeds and reapers gather crops.

Combines are machines that harvest grains like wheat.

# Problems That Farmers Face

Crops and animals are ruined by floods and **droughts**. A drought means there is not enough rainwater for crops and animals. A flood is too much rain.

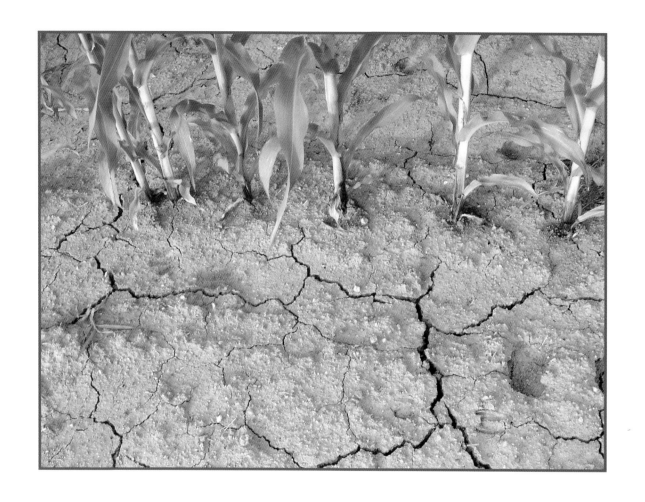

   Crops and animals are also hurt
by contagious diseases that farmers
call **pestilence**.

# Farming and Science

Scientists are trying to improve the way crops grow to make more food to feed our growing world.

They are trying to grow **genetically modified foods** that can resist pests and disease.

# The Future of Farming

The future of farming is exciting! One day we may have nutritious new foods that can feed all the people of the world.

# Glossary

**crops** (KROPS) — plants grown on farms to be sold for food, clothing, and fuel

**drought** (DRAUT) — a time without rainfall

**genetically modified foods** (jen ET tick lee  MOD eh fyed  FOODS) — foods with changed genes that control their structure and characteristics

**harvest** (HAR vist) — the gathering of grown food crops

**livestock** (LYVE stock) — animals, including cattle, sheep, goats, and pigs

**pestilence** (PES till ense) — contagious diseases that affect plants and animals

# Index

## FURTHER READING

Wellington, Monica. Apple Farmer Annie. Puffin, 2004.

Wheeler, Lisa. Farmer Dale's Red Pickup Truck. Voyager Books, 2006.

Whybrow, Ian. Little Farmer Joe. Kingfisher, 2003.

## WEBSITES TO VISIT

Because Internet links change so often, Fitzgerald Books has developed an online list of websites related to the subject of this book. This site is updated regularly. Please use this link to access the list:  www.fitzgeraldbookslinks.com/ch/far

## ABOUT THE AUTHOR

Sandy Sepehri is an honors graduate from the University of Central Florida. She has authored several children's books and is a columnist for a parents' magazine.

Chantrell Creek Elementary